The Sculptor of Beaver Pond

Written by
Jeff Kallet

Illustrated by
Pat Whittaker

In the grassy meadow near Beaver Pond a young beaver was resting on his back. His eyes were squinted as he watched a parade of puffy clouds march above him in the sunny sky. In between his beaver teeth he nibbled on a stick.

A fuzzy bumblebee buzzed around him, then it landed on the tip of his nose. He stopped for a moment to stare cross-eyed at the bee. Then it rose and buzzed away.

The beaver sighed and went back to his nibbling.

"Buford" was the beaver's name. Like all beavers in the world, Buford
had a pair of long teeth, a flat tail and a thick, lovely coat of fur. But one
thing set Buford apart from other beavers: he didn't like his work.

Buford wasn't lazy, though. He worked in the woods with the other beavers. He chewed the bottoms of trees from morning until night, tipping them down and dragging them to Beaver Pond. He helped to build dams and beaver lodges.

Buford just thought beaver work was, well . . . boring.

One day Buford stood up on a tree stump and began nibbling away. His father walked up behind him to see what was the matter.

"Son, what in the world are you doing?" he asked.

Surprised, Buford smiled nervously. "Ooops, nothing—I mean—sorry. Bye," he sputtered, before quickly waddling away through some ferns, feeling very embarrassed.

Buford's father stood with his hands on his hips, looking at the stump. Then he bent down to look closer. He saw a wooden bumblebee carved on top of a wooden mushroom cap.

That night at home, after dinner, Buford's father said to his wife, "I'm worried about our son. Guess what I found him doing in the woods today?"

"Hmmn, let me guess," answered Buford's mother. "Carving?"

"Carving is not what I'd call it," said Buford's father. "I'd call it a waste of time."

"Oh, I wouldn't worry," Buford's mother said. "He's just a dreamy beaver. The creative type."

She held up one of Buford's many branch carvings she collected. "There's a creative streak in my family, you know. My Uncle Roger—"

"I know, I know, Uncle Roger, the great beaver lodge builder," moaned Buford's father.

It was another warm, breezy autumn day at Beaver Pond. Buford was back in the woods, leaning against a tree, when suddenly everything became quiet. On the dirt path that ran beside the pond, a hiker had stopped walking. She took off her backpack and sat down on a rock.

Buford watched as she opened her pack, took out a notebook and began drawing with a pencil.

"What could she be doing?" Buford wondered. "She's just . . . sitting there," he thought.

She sat on the rock for a long, long time.

Many minutes later, the hiker stood up and stretched. She stuffed the
notebook into her backpack, threw it over her shoulder, and started to walk
away. But as she was leaving, Buford saw her notebook slip from the
backpack and fall to the path.

When the girl was out of sight, Buford scuttled down to the path.
He was very curious.

Inside the notebook, Buford found pages and pages filled with amazing drawings. There were pictures of things he'd never seen before, like a motorcycle, a vase in a window, and a very large drawing of someone's nose.

"What's all of this?!" Buford exclaimed. He was baffled, but quite interested.

The hiker's notebook also had drawings of statues, a Siamese cat, the steps of an apartment building, a big bowl overflowing with fruit . . . .

It was a whole new world to Buford.

With one foot holding down two pages, and with his eyes focused on a single drawing, Buford dug his teeth into a nearby stump. He nibbled a bit here. And he cut a bit there.

He gnawed and he chewed, he shaved and he bit, until a small pile of woodchips surrounded the stump, which had begun to resemble a large, magnificent human nose!

Although he had never ever seen a human nose, Buford was able to chisel away at the stump until it looked just like the nose in the notebook.

While he was putting on the finishing touches, a group of beavers came waddling by at the end of their workday. They stopped when they came to this impressive new addition to Beaver Pond.

"Uhh . . . hi, fellas," said Buford, as he wiggled out from a giant wooden nostril, brushing chips from his fur. "I was just, uh, carving! Carving this—stump!"

The other beavers didn't say a thing. They just stared.

Then, a curious thing happened.

"Wonderful!" said one beaver.

"Fantastic!" said another.

"What a talent!" said a third.

Before long, all the beavers decided that Buford, with his unique talent for carving wood, should make it his full-time job to sculpt the stumps, logs and old trees of Beaver Pond. Magically, their home began to look like a museum.

Buford's mother, and even his father, were proud of their talented son.

And that's the happy story of how a bored little beaver became the great Sculptor of Beaver Pond.